TULSA CITY-COUNTY LIBRARY

W9-BJS-301

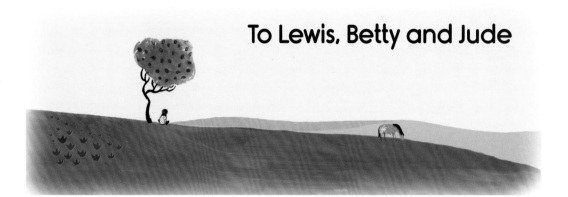

To Lewis, Betty and Jude

Starfish Bay® Children's Books
An imprint of Starfish Bay Publishing
www.starfishbaypublishing.com

TAMLIN'S GREAT ADVENTURE

© Victoria Byron, 2020
ISBN 978-1-76036-084-9
First Published 2020
Printed in China

This book is copyright. Apart from any fair dealing for the purpose of private study, research, criticism or review, as permitted under the Copyright Act, no part of this publication may be reproduced or transmitted in any form or by any means without the prior written permission of the publisher.

Sincere thanks to Elyse Williams from Starfish Bay Children's Books for her creative efforts in preparing this edition for publication.

Tamlin's Great Adventure

Victoria Byron

Tamlin was a very lucky horse. He lived in a field with his best friend, Ruby. They played together all day long, and life was perfect.

The field had soft grass,

sweet smelling flowers
and soothing birdsong.

"This field is the best place in
the world," said Ruby, and
Tamlin agreed.

But one day, a little bird told Tamlin about
the Wide World...

...and Tamlin began to dream.

For the first time ever, he wondered what was beyond the beautiful field.

So, one moonlit night, he left...

...and by morning, he was far, far away.
"I'm going on a great adventure," he thought, and deep down in his tummy he felt a little spark of happiness.

Tamlin sailed to a tropical island,

with scorching sun, soft sandy beaches...

and colourful, cackling creatures.
"This island is the best place in the world,"
he thought.

Tamlin swam in the island's balmy blue oceans...

and jogged through its jabbering jungles.

But although the island looked like a painting, it was a lonely place. The swish of the ocean and the chattering of the jungle were the only sounds. Tamlin wondered what was beyond the island.

So, he sailed to a huge city, with towering buildings.
"Wow," thought Tamlin. "This city is the best place in the world."

The people in the city were polished and perfect,

and Tamlin saw things he just couldn't believe.

But although he was surrounded by people, Tamlin felt lonelier than ever. Everyone was in such a hurry and didn't notice him at all. He wondered what was beyond the big city.

Tamlin travelled north, south, east and west.
He crossed vast deserts and sailed the seven seas.
He climbed the highest mountains until he could
climb no more,

but nowhere was just right.

And then, suddenly, he realised what was wrong!

How could he have forgotten something so important?

It was time to go home...

...home, to the most fabulous, wonderful, fantastical, glorious field.

And back to his best friend Ruby!

The grass in the field was still as soft,

the flowers still as sweet smelling

and the birdsong still as soothing.

"This field is the best place in the whole wide world,"
said Ruby, and Tamlin agreed.

But every now and again, especially when the moon gets silvery, Tamlin begins to dream...

...of great adventures, but this time with Ruby!